ALBERT IS NOT SCARED

by **Eleanor May** • Illustrated by **Deborah Melmon**

THE KANE PRESS / NEW YORK

For Egan—hope you are "amoused"! —E.M.

Acknowledgments: We wish to thank the following people for their helpful advice and review of the material contained in this book: Susan Longo, Early Childhood and Elementary School Teacher, Mamaroneck, NY; and Rebeka Eston Salemi, Kindergarten Teacher, Lincoln School, Lincoln, MA.

Special thanks to Susan Longo for providing the Fun Activities in the back of this book.

Library of Congress Cataloging-in-Publication Data

May, Eleanor.
Albert is NOT scared / by Eleanor May ; illustrated by Deborah Melmon.
pages cm. — (Mouse math)
"With fun activities!"
Summary: On his first visit to the mouse amusement park, Albert claims he is not afraid, he simply does not like rides that go up and down, left and right, or around and around, but things change when he and his sister Wanda accidentally ride the roller coaster.
ISBN 978-1-57565-628-1 (library reinforced binding : alk. paper) — ISBN 978-1-57565-629-8 (pbk. : alk. paper) — ISBN 978-1-57565-630-4 (e-book)
[1. Mice—Fiction. 2. Amusement parks—Fiction. 3. Mathematics—Fiction.] I. Melmon, Deborah, illustrator. II. Title.
PZ7.M4513Alc 2013
[E]—dc23   2012051090

1 3 5 7 9 10 8 6 4 2

First published in the United States of America in 2013 by Kane Press, Inc.
Printed in the United States of America
WOZ0713

Book Design: Edward Miller

Mouse Math is a registered trademark of Kane Press, Inc.

Visit us online at **www.kanepress.com**

 Like us on Facebook
facebook.com/kanepress

Follow us on Twitter
@KanePress

Dear Parent/Educator,

"I can't do math." Every child (or grownup!) who says these words has at some point along the way felt intimidated by math. For young children who are just being introduced to the subject, we wanted to create a world in which math was not simply numbers on a page, but a part of life—an adventure!

Enter Albert and Wanda, two little mice who live in the walls of a People House. Children will be swept along with this irrepressible duo and their merry band of friends as they tackle mouse-sized problems and dilemmas. (And sometimes *cat-sized* problems and dilemmas!)

Each book in the **MOUSE MATH®** series provides a fresh take on a basic math concept. The mice discover solutions as they, for instance, use position words while teaching a pet snail to do tricks or count the alarmingly large number of friends they've invited over on a rainy day—and, lo and behold, they are doing math!

Math educators who specialize in early childhood learning used their expertise to make sure each title would be as helpful as possible to young kids—and to their parents and teachers. Fun activities at the end of the books and on our website encourage children to think and talk about math in ways that will make each concept clear and memorable.

As with our award-winning Math Matters® series, our aim is to captivate children's imaginations by drawing them into the story, and so into the math at the heart of each adventure. It is our hope that kids will want to hear and read the **MOUSE MATH** stories again and again and that, as they grow up, they will approach math with enthusiasm and see it as an invaluable tool for navigating the world they live in.

Sincerely,

Joanne Kane

Joanne E. Kane
Publisher

Albert had never been to the amousement park before.

"You'll *love* it," his sister, Wanda, said.

"Which ride should we go on first?" she asked.
"Daredevil Drop?"

DARE DEVIL DROP

TICKETS

Albert watched the mice strap themselves into their seats. Slowly, the ride carried them **up**.

Up

"AAAAAAAAAAAAAAAAAAHHHH!" the mice shrieked as they came **down**.

"I don't want to go on that ride," Albert said.

"Don't be scared," Wanda told him. "It's fun!"

"I'm not scared." Albert crossed his paws.
"I just don't like rides that go up and down."

Down

"How about the pirate ship, then?" Wanda asked.

The pirate ship swung **left**.
All the mice screamed.

Left

The pirate ship swung **right**.
All the mice screamed again.

Albert said, "I don't like things that go side to side."

Pi-Rat Ship

Right

Wanda took him to the motor boats,
but Albert didn't want to go **across** the pond.
"The water isn't deep," his sister pointed out.

"The water doesn't scare me," Albert said.
"I just don't like rides that go across things, that's all."

Across

The Mole Hole ride went **through** a long, dark tunnel. Wanda sighed. "I bet you don't like rides that go through things."

Albert said, "How did you know?"

Through

He wouldn't even try the carousel.

"You don't have to go up and down," Wanda explained.

"The birds go up and down, but not the cats.

The cats don't move at all."

Mousey-G

Albert eyed the cats' sharp claws and teeth.
"I'm not going on the carousel," he said.
"I don't like rides that go **around**."

Around

Wanda bought Albert a popsicle and led him **toward** a picnic table.

"Aren't you going to try *any* of the rides?" she asked.

Toward

Albert pointed. "What does that one do?"

Chew Chew Train

"It's a train. You ride it," Wanda said.

"Does it go **backward**?" Albert asked.

"No, the Chew Chew Train only goes **forward**.
And not very fast."

"I like things that only go forward," Albert said.

Backward Forward

Albert pulled Wanda **toward** the train. "This must be where we get in line," he told her.

Chew Chew Train

TAIL TWISTER

ENTRANCE

When their turn came, Albert said, "Let's sit in front."

Wanda looked at the train cars.
"Albert," she said. "Something seems—"

"Come *on*!" Albert said.

As they strapped themselves in, Wanda said, "Albert, I'm not sure we're on the Chew Chew Train. It doesn't look the same."

Before Albert could answer, the ride started.

The cars moved **forward**.

Albert stared at the track ahead.

"Wanda . . . did we get on the *roller coaster*?"

Wanda squeezed Albert's paw.

They headed **up** . . .

And up . . .

And up.

21

At the top, the cars paused.
Wanda peeked over the edge.
"Albert!" She clutched his paw. "Whatever you do,
don't look—"

Albert and Wanda zoomed into a curve.
They tilted **left**.

They tilted **right**.

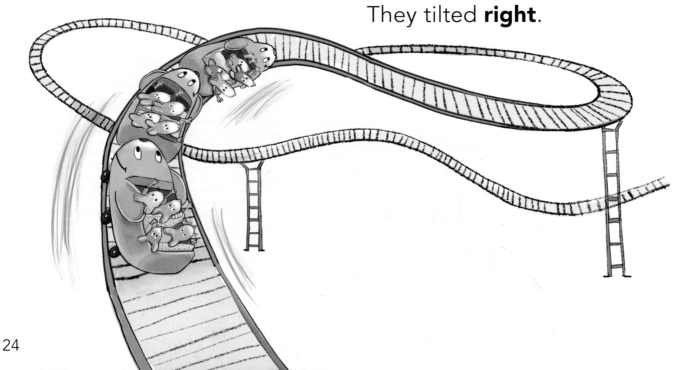

They raced **around** a loop.

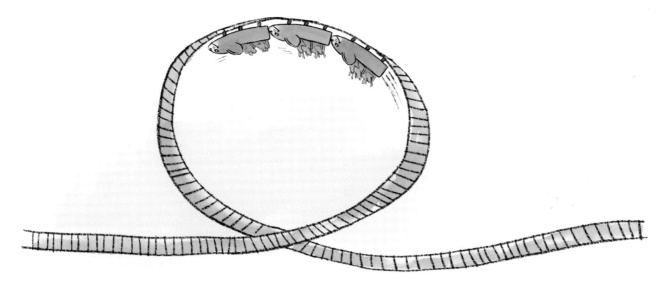

They barreled **through** a long, dark tunnel.

At last, they came to the end of the ride.
The cars slowed, then stopped.

Albert didn't move.
Wanda unbuckled him.
She took his paw and led him **away** from the ride.

Away

TAIL TWISTER

RANCE

Wanda sank down on a bench.
"I can't believe we rode the biggest
roller coaster in the park!" she gasped.
"I was too terrified to squeak!"

"I wasn't scared," Albert said.

Wanda smiled. "I know. You're never scared.
You just don't like it when a ride goes
up and **down** and all **around**!"

"I don't like it," Albert said. . . .

"I *LOVE* IT! Let's do it again!"

Albert Is NOT Scared supports children's understanding of **direction words**, an important topic in early math learning. Use the activities below to extend the math topic and to reinforce children's early reading skills.

🐭 ENGAGE

Remind children that the cover of a book can tell them a lot about the story inside.

▷ Before reading the story, show children the front cover while covering up the title. Ask them what this story may be about. You may wish to record their predictions and refer back to them at the end of the story.

▷ Now uncover the title and read it aloud. Ask children how they think Albert might be feeling. Ask: *How many of you have been to an amusement park? Was it fun or was it scary?* Say to the children: *Now let's read the story and find out what Albert may be scared of!*

🐭 LOOK BACK

▷ After reading the story, ask children to recall what rides Albert encountered in the *amousement* park. Make a list of the rides on the left side of a large sheet of paper (e.g., Daredevil Drop, pirate ship, motor boats, etc.).

▷ Now ask the children to recall in which direction each ride moved: **up, down, left, right, across, through, around, forward**. (Remind children that the roller coaster moved in a *lot* of different directions! Can they recall each one?) Record the answer(s) for each ride on the right side of the paper.

▷ Now read the story again and be sure that all the rides in the story are included on the list formed by the children. If not, add each ride (and corresponding direction word) as Albert encounters it.

🐭 TRY THIS!

Build a Mini Amusement Park!

▸ On a table top, gather several toy cars and a variety of materials such as: a tube (for a car to go through), a plastic dish (that spins around), a ruler propped on a block to form a slide (for a car to roll up and down), blocks to form a bridge (for a car to drive across), etc.

▸ Have children use their imaginations to create this "mini-amusement park." As they play, be sure to ask: *What direction is the car going in?* Challenge children to create objects and obstacles that will utilize every direction word from the story.

▸ You may wish to find a safe place to store this project so that children can enjoy adding to their work as days go by.

🐭 THINK!

Let's Play "Albert Says!" (This game is similar to Simon Says, but no one gets called out!)

▸ Print out and cut apart the Direction Strips at www.kanepress.com/mousemath-direction.html. Hand a strip to each child (you may need to print some duplicates).

▸ Using the word bank and strips provided, have each child think up their own "direction" for the class to follow by filling in the appropriate direction word on his or her strip. For example: "Albert says: Take two hops ___[forward]___ !"

▸ Collect the completed strips and gather the children in an open area in the room.

▸ Read each strip aloud and have the children follow each direction. (You may wish to include some of your own direction strips in the mix!)

▸ Have fun playing until all the strips have been read at least once. Encourage children to take turns being the reader!

Bonus: For extra fun, make up another set of direction strips and take the game outdoors—to a playground!

◆ **FOR MORE ACTIVITIES** ◆

visit www.kanepress.com/mousemath-activities.html